This book belongs to

ZZc

LADYBIRD BOOKS
UK | USA | Canada | Ireland | Australia | India | New Zealand | South Africa

Ladybird Books is part of the Penguin Random House group of companies
whose addresses can be found at global.penguinrandomhouse.com.

www.penguin.co.uk   www.puffin.co.uk   www.ladybird.co.uk

 Penguin
Random House
UK

First published 2021
001

Licensed by

Printed in China

The authorized representative in the EEA is Penguin Random House Ireland,
Morrison Chambers, 32 Nassau Street, Dublin D02 YH68

A CIP catalogue record for this book is available from the British Library

ISBN: 978-0-241-47652-9

All correspondence to:
Ladybird Books, Penguin Random House Children's
One Embassy Gardens, 8 Viaduct Gardens, London SW11 7BW

MIX
Paper from
responsible sources
FSC www.fsc.org   **FSC® C018179**

Peppa's Countdown to Bedtime

Granny and Grandpa Pig were visiting
Peppa and George's house. They'd had lots
of fun together, but it was getting late . . .

"Come on, little ones," said Daddy Pig. "Let's get you ready for bed."
"Can we play the Countdown to Bedtime game with Granny and
Grandpa?" asked Peppa. "Pleeeaase?"

"That's a lovely idea, Peppa," said Mummy Pig. "Why don't you tell Granny and Grandpa Pig how to play it?"

"First, you count ten things, then nine things,
then eight things . . . all the way down to one thing,
before you go to bed!" explained Peppa.
"That sounds like a game we used to play with your
mummy when she was your age," said Granny Pig.

"Who's going to start the counting down?" asked Grandpa Pig. "Me!" cried Peppa excitedly. "I know! First, let's jump in **ten** muddy puddles!"

Peppa and George raced outside, closely followed by Grandpa Pig. They found **ten** very muddy puddles, perfect for jumping in!

Splash!

Splash!

Splash!

Splash!

Splash!

Splash!

10

Peppa, George and Grandpa Pig jumped in **ten** *very muddy* puddles. Everyone was laughing and covered in mud. "Hee! Hee! Hee!"

Splash! Splash!

Splash!

Splash!

"That's **ten** muddy puddles jumped in!" said Peppa. "What's next?"

"It's starting to get dark," whispered Grandpa Pig. "Before we go inside, shall we use my torch to see if we can spot nine night-time creatures?"

"Oooh, yes!" Peppa whispered back.
Peppa, George and Grandpa Pig tiptoed around
the garden looking for night-time creatures . . .

Suddenly, George spotted lots of little hedgehogs scuttling across the grass. "Heggy-hogs!" he cried, pointing.

9

Peppa, George and Grandpa Pig counted **nine** cute hedgehogs. "Great night-time detective work!" said Grandpa Pig.

"That's **nine** night-time creatures spotted!" said Peppa. "What's next?"

Tweet! Tweet! Tweet! Tweet!

Tweet!

George shone the torch up at the sky.
"Tweet-tweet!" he said.
"Look! George has found **eight**
little birds flying to their nests,"
said Peppa. "Night-night, little birds."

8

Tweet!
Tweet!
Tweet!

"Well done, George,"
said Grandpa Pig.
Peppa and George
waved goodnight to
eight little birds
flying to their nests.

"That's **eight** little
birds waved to!" said
Peppa. "What's next?"

"I think it's time *you* flew home, too,"
said Mummy Pig, coming outside.
Peppa, George and Grandpa Pig
pretended to be birds flying back home.

In the living room, Granny Pig said, "I see seven
toy monkeys that need to be tidied away."
Peppa and George picked up seven toy monkeys
and put them in the basket.
"Goodnight, monkeys!" said Peppa.

7

"That's seven toy monkeys tidied
away!" said Peppa. "What's next?"

"Peppa! George!" called Daddy Pig.
Everyone rushed to the kitchen to find Daddy Pig
with six glasses of warm milk.
"Here are six bedtime drinks!" said Daddy Pig.

6

"Yummy! Thank you, Daddy," said Peppa, lifting her head up to show everyone her milk moustache.
"You're welcome, Peppa," said Daddy Pig.

"That's six glasses of a yummy bedtime drink drunk!" said Peppa. "What's next?"

"Shall we get you all cleaned up?"
Granny Pig asked Peppa and George.
"Bath time!" cheered Peppa. "Hooray!"
In the bathroom, Granny Pig spotted
five rubber ducks in need of a wash.

Splash! Splash! Splash!

Splash! Splash!

5

Peppa and George had lots of fun bathing
with the five rubber ducks . . . and
splashing Granny and Grandpa Pig, too!

"It's time for the c̶ bed now," said Gran
"Night-night, **five** lit said Peppa.

"That's **five** rubber ducks nice and clean!"
said Peppa. "What's next?"

Mummy and Daddy Pig came to help Peppa and
George get into their pyjamas and brush their teeth.
"Oh no!" gasped Peppa.
"What's wrong?" asked Daddy Pig.

"We need something for number four," said Peppa,
"but George and I only have two toothbrushes."

"Don't worry," said Mummy Pig. "Daddy and I will brush our teeth, too. Then we'll have one, two, three . . ."
"Four!" finished Peppa. "*Brush, brush, brush, brush!*"

4

After they were finished, Peppa said, "That's **four** brushy toothbrushes brushed with. What's next?"

Grandpa Pig went to close the curtains
in Peppa and George's bedroom.

3

When they looked out of the window, Peppa and
George counted **three** stars shining in the night sky.

"Look, George!" cried Peppa. "**Three** twinkling stars!
Let's pretend we're in a rocket, exploring outer space!"

Twinkle!

Twinkle!

Twinkle!

"That's **three** twinkling stars counted!"
said Peppa. "What's next?"

Grandpa Pig helped George into bed. "Peppa, you tuck in Teddy. George, you tuck in Mr Dinosaur. Then that's two favourite toys ready to sleep!"

"That's two favourite toys all tucked in!" said Peppa. "What's next?"

2

"Ahhh," said Granny Pig. "We have a very special number **one** for you."
"We do?" said Grandpa Pig. Then he thought for a moment. "Oh yes, of course," he said. "We have **one** very special bedtime story for you both."

"Hooray!" cheered Peppa and George. They loved bedtime stories.

Peppa and George were all cuddled up and cosy in bed when Granny Pig started their **one** very special bedtime story . . .

1

"Once upon a time," began Granny Pig, *very* quietly and *very* slowly, "there were two little piggies who . . .

jumped in **ten** muddy puddles,

spotted **nine** night-time creatures,

waved to **eight** little birds,

tidied **seven** toy monkeys,

shared **six** bedtime drinks ..."

"... bathed with **five** rubber ducks,

found **four** brushy toothbrushes,

counted **three** twinkling stars,

tucked in **two** favourite toys ..."

As Peppa and George closed their eyes, Granny Pig whispered, "... and listened to **one** *very special* bedtime story. Night-night, little ones."

Peppa and George were so tired from playing the Countdown to Bedtime game, they had fallen asleep!

Snore!

Snore!

Mummy and Daddy Pig came in to say goodnight. "Ahhh," said Mummy Pig, seeing Peppa and George fast asleep. "You can always *count* on the Countdown to Bedtime game!"
"You can indeed!" said Granny Pig, looking over at Grandpa Pig . . .

. . . who had fallen asleep, too.
Mummy Pig, Daddy Pig and Granny Pig all laughed. "Ha! Ha! Ha!"
Peppa and George love counting down to bedtime. Everyone loves counting down to bedtime!